The Red Hen

by Bobby Lynn Maslen
pictures by John R. Maslen

Scholastic Inc.
New York • Toronto • London • Auckland • Sydney • Mexico City • New Delhi • Hong Kong • Buenos Aires

Available Bob Books®:

Set 1: Beginning Readers — With consistent new sounds added gradually, your new reader is gently introduced to all the letters of the alphabet. They can soon say, "I read the whole book!®"

Set 2: Advancing Beginners — The use of three-letter words and consistent vowel sounds in slightly longer stories build skill and confidence.

Set 3: Word Families — Consonant blends, endings and a few sight words advance reading skills while the use of word families keep reading manageable.

Set 4: Complex Words — Longer books and complex words engage young readers as proficiency advances.

Set 5: Long Vowels — Silent e and other vowel blends build young readers' vocabulary and aptitude.

Bob Books® Collections:

Collection 1 — Includes Set 1: Beginning Readers and part of Set 2: Advancing Beginners

Collection 2 — Includes part of Set 2: Advancing Beginners and Set 3: Word Families

Collection 3 — Includes Set 4: Complex Words and Set 5: Long Vowels

Ask for Bob Books at your local bookstore, or visit www.bobbooks.com.

ISBN 0-545-02685-7

6 5 4 3 2   10 11/0

Printed in China   68
This edition first printing, September 2007

Ben met a red hen.

The hen was wet.

The hen was sad.

The hen was not OK.

Ben put the hen in his bed.

The hen had a nap.

The hen sat up.

"Buc-a-buc! Buc-a-buc-buc!"

The hen was OK.

Ben put the hen out.

Then Ben saw the bed had
ten eggs.

OK for the hen.
OK for Ben.

The End

List of 27 words in <u>The Red Hen</u>

Short Vowels

<u>a</u>	<u>e</u>	<u>i</u>	<u>o</u>	<u>u</u>	<u>sight</u>
had	bed	in	for	buc	a
nap	Ben		not	up	his
sad	eggs				OK
sat	end				out
	hen				put
	met				saw
	red				the
	ten				was
	then				
	wet				

67 total words in *The Red Hen*